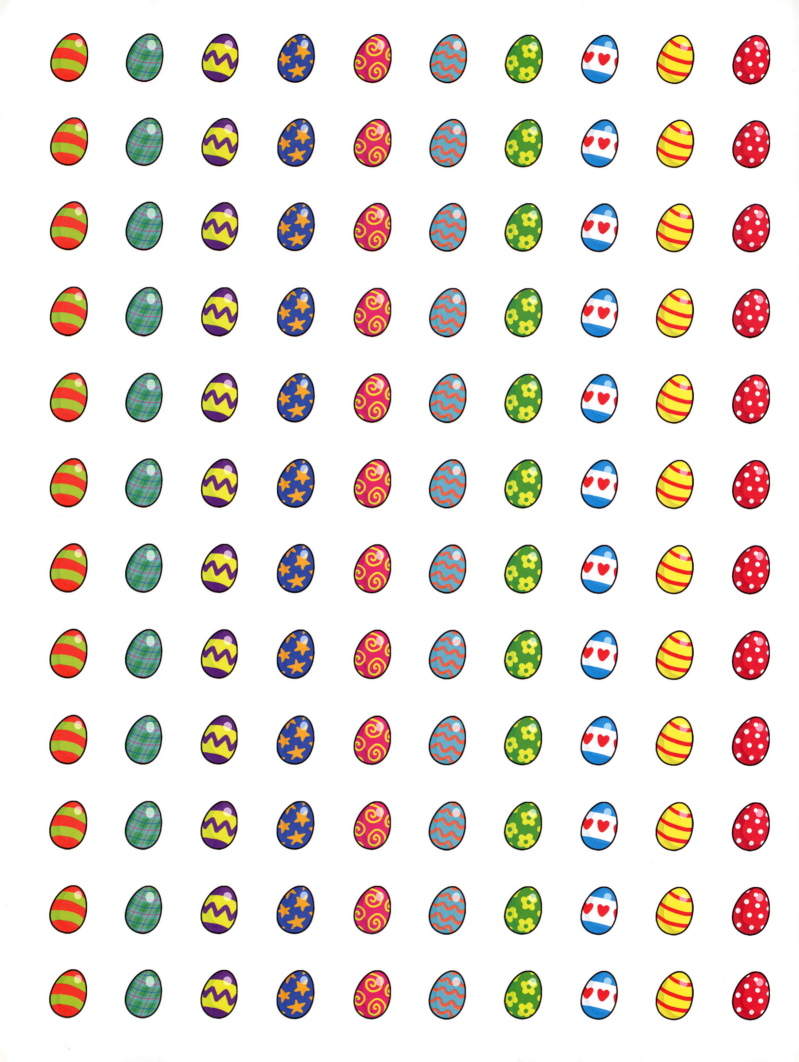

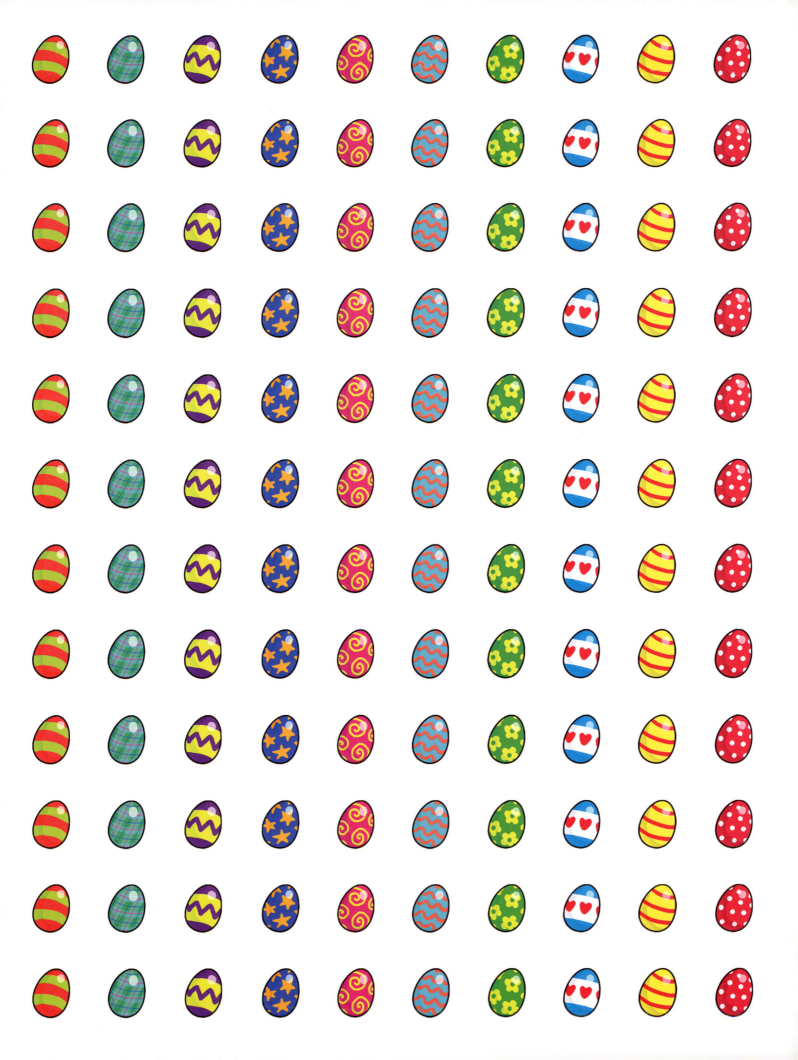

WHERE'S THE BUNNY?

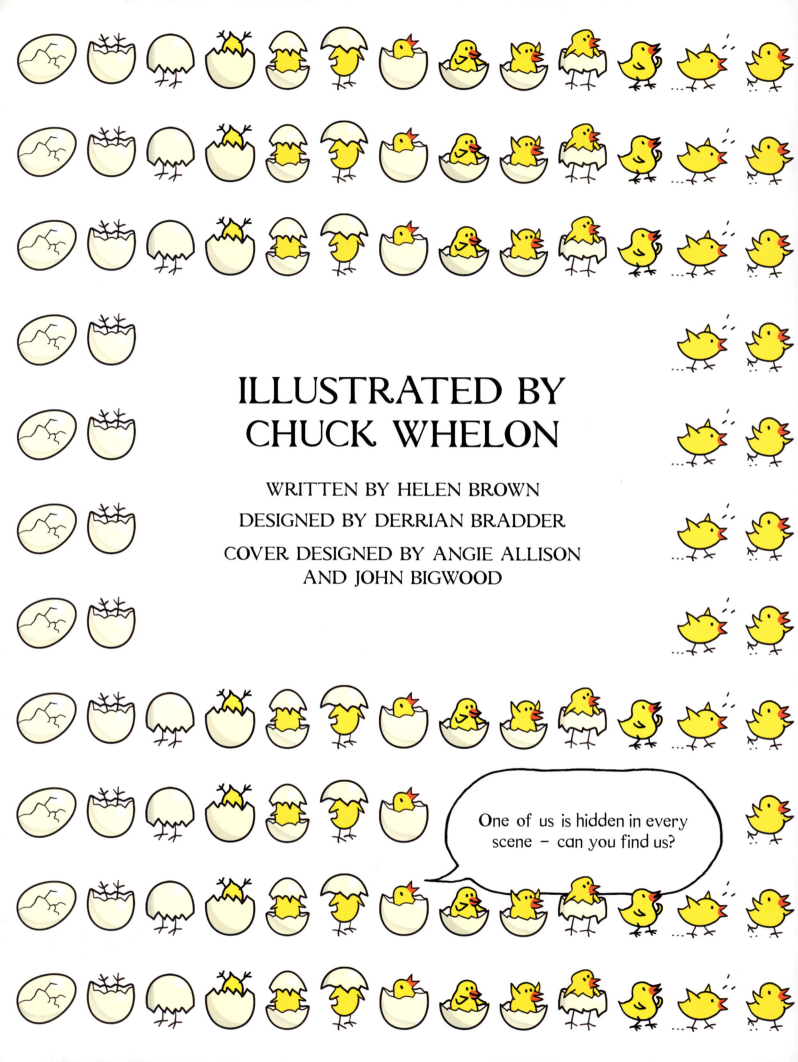

ILLUSTRATED BY CHUCK WHELON

WRITTEN BY HELEN BROWN

DESIGNED BY DERRIAN BRADDER

COVER DESIGNED BY ANGIE ALLISON
AND JOHN BIGWOOD

One of us is hidden in every scene – can you find us?

WHERE'S THE BUNNY?

Buster Books

Look closely as we appear in this order in the book.

A Workshop in Easterland

Easter is fast approaching. The rabbits are busy in their workshop decorating chocolate eggs. They can't wait to fill their baskets with these tasty treasures and deliver them to children around the world.

But disaster strikes – a whole batch of eggs have fallen down the rabbit hole and landed in Fairyland. Without them, the rabbits won't be able to deliver all the eggs on time. They've sent Bunny, their expert egg hunter, to bring the batch back to Easterland.

Can you find Bunny and the ten chocolate eggs hidden in each magical picture? Take an enchanting journey through Fairyland and get ready to search high and low.

You can find the answers, plus extra things to spot, at the back of the book.

The Missing Eggs

Look closely at the ten chocolate eggs that have gone missing.
Don't forget to spot a chick in every scene too.

Cinderella

Cinderella has lost her glass slipper at the ball. She's in a rush to get to the golden carriage before the clock strikes midnight and the magic spell is broken. There's not enough time to help Cinderella as Bunny must hop to it and gather up the chocolate eggs.

Can you find Bunny and the ten missing eggs?

Hansel and Gretel

Hansel and Gretel have stumbled across a cottage made of gingerbread. They are too distracted by the tasty sweets to notice the chocolate eggs, but that won't last long. Bunny needs to track down the eggs before Hansel and Gretel get their sticky hands on them.

Can you find Bunny and the ten missing eggs?

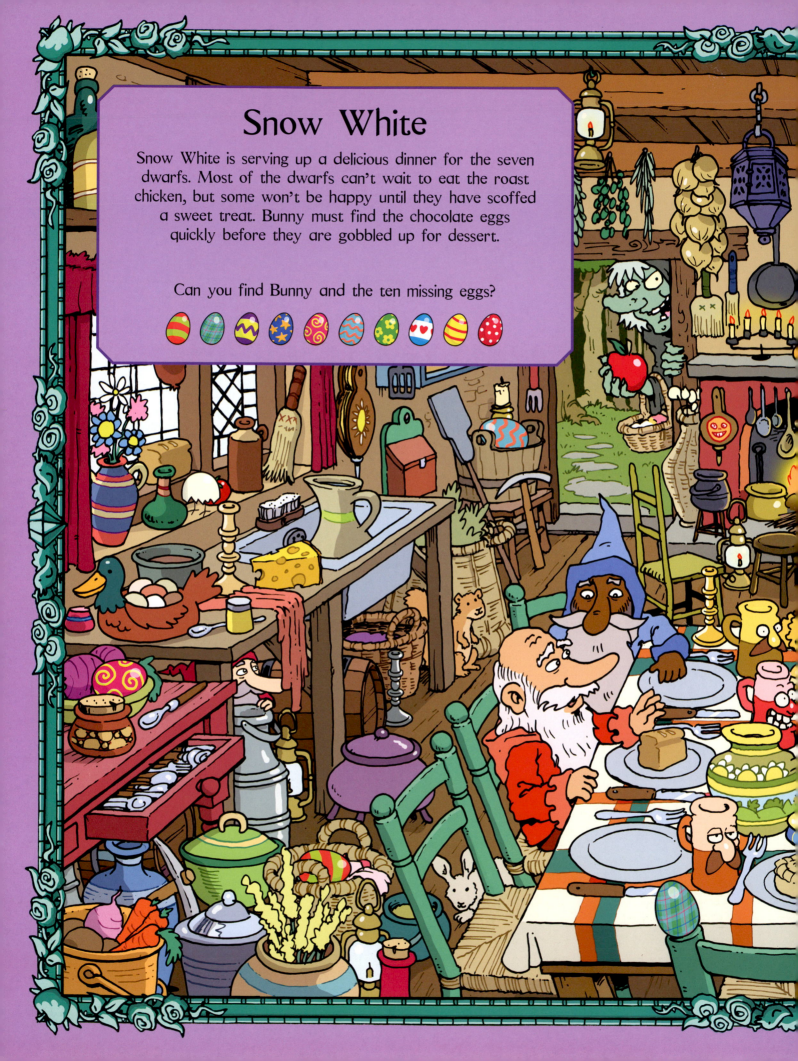

Snow White

Snow White is serving up a delicious dinner for the seven dwarfs. Most of the dwarfs can't wait to eat the roast chicken, but some won't be happy until they have scoffed a sweet treat. Bunny must find the chocolate eggs quickly before they are gobbled up for dessert.

Can you find Bunny and the ten missing eggs?

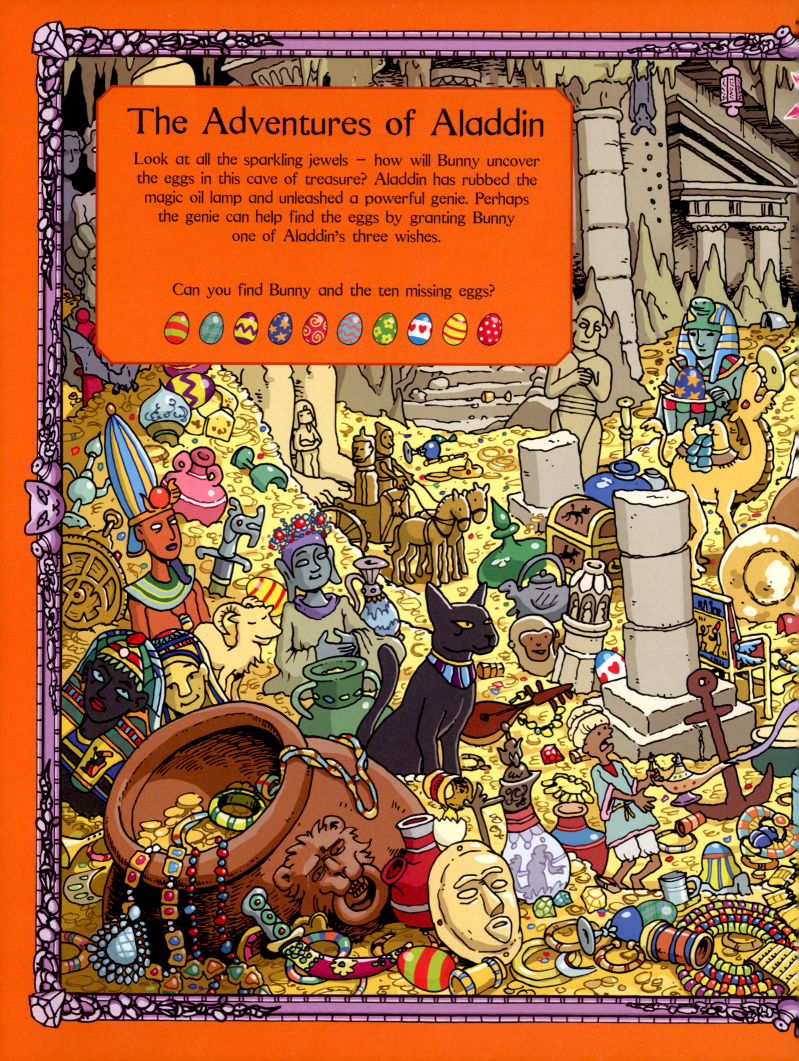

The Adventures of Aladdin

Look at all the sparkling jewels — how will Bunny uncover the eggs in this cave of treasure? Aladdin has rubbed the magic oil lamp and unleashed a powerful genie. Perhaps the genie can help find the eggs by granting Bunny one of Aladdin's three wishes.

Can you find Bunny and the ten missing eggs?

The Princess and the Pea

The princess has had an awful night's sleep after the queen put a pea under her mattress. Poor Bunny is hoping that the queen didn't put any of the chocolate eggs under there as well. The workshop in Easterland wouldn't be happy to receive a broken egg.

Can you find Bunny and the ten missing eggs?

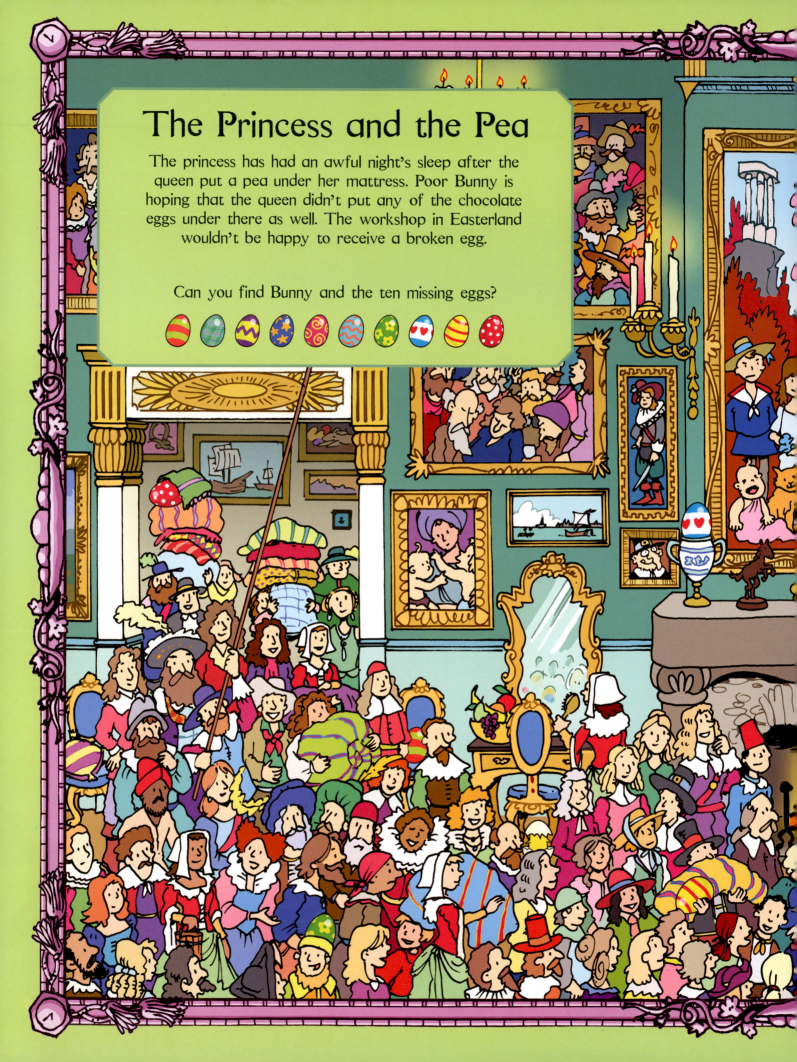

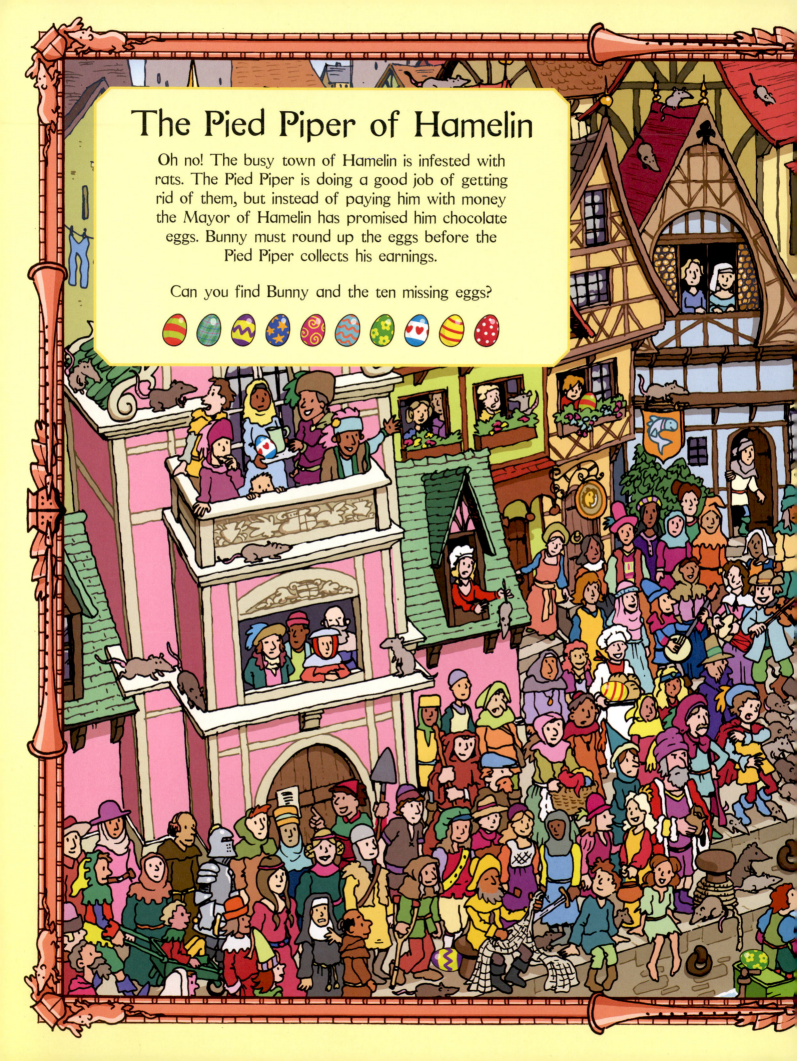

The Pied Piper of Hamelin

Oh no! The busy town of Hamelin is infested with rats. The Pied Piper is doing a good job of getting rid of them, but instead of paying him with money the Mayor of Hamelin has promised him chocolate eggs. Bunny must round up the eggs before the Pied Piper collects his earnings.

Can you find Bunny and the ten missing eggs?

Sleeping Beauty

Bunny has managed to sneak past the snoozing guards and hop over the castle walls. The prince is about to give Sleeping Beauty a kiss, which will wake up the entire kingdom – and they have been asleep for a hundred years. Bunny is starting to worry about how hungry all these people will be once the spell is broken.

Can you find Bunny and the ten missing eggs?

Pinocchio

Pinocchio the puppet has sprung to life. He has told Bunny that he hasn't seen any of the chocolate eggs in Geppetto's workshop. Bunny is not convinced that Pinocchio is telling the truth. It's a struggle to believe the boy when his wooden nose keeps growing like that!

Can you find Bunny and the ten missing eggs?

The Little Mermaid

Bunny has taken a dive to the bottom of the ocean and is surrounded by plenty of friendly fish. The Little Mermaid and the Sea King have oodles of gold and pearls hidden in their treasure trove. But there's no time to stop and admire the jewels as Bunny has more important chocolate treasure to search for.

Can you find Bunny and the ten missing eggs?

The Frog Prince

The shy princess should be careful when throwing her magic golden ball in the air. She's standing very close to the pond and if it falls in the frog may magically transform into a prince. Bunny doesn't like surprises and won't stick around to see how this story ends.

Can you find Bunny and the ten missing eggs?

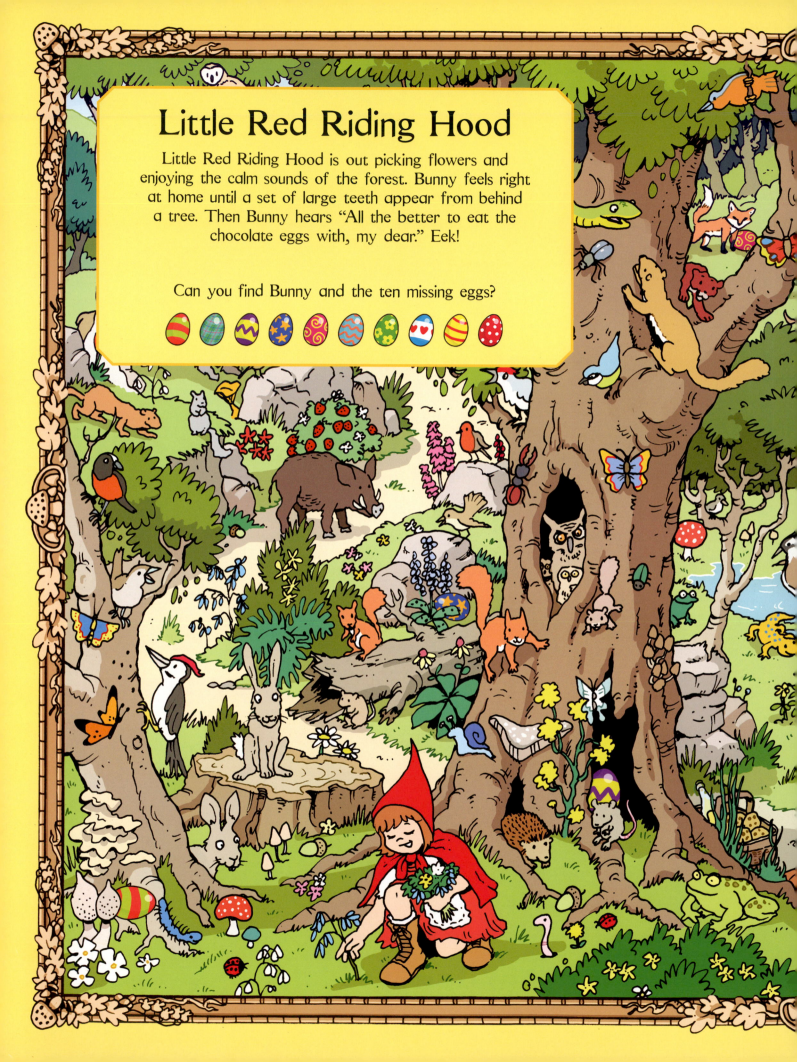

Little Red Riding Hood

Little Red Riding Hood is out picking flowers and enjoying the calm sounds of the forest. Bunny feels right at home until a set of large teeth appear from behind a tree. Then Bunny hears "All the better to eat the chocolate eggs with, my dear." Eek!

Can you find Bunny and the ten missing eggs?

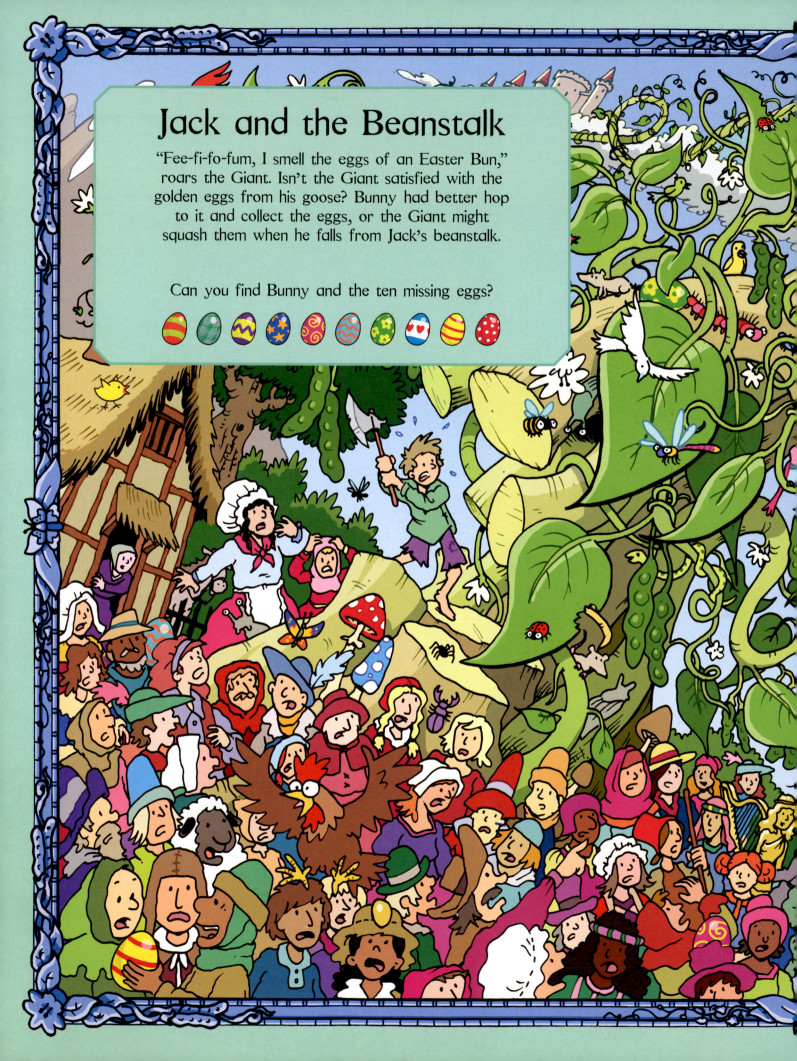

Jack and the Beanstalk

"Fee-fi-fo-fum, I smell the eggs of an Easter Bun," roars the Giant. Isn't the Giant satisfied with the golden eggs from his goose? Bunny had better hop to it and collect the eggs, or the Giant might squash them when he falls from Jack's beanstalk.

Can you find Bunny and the ten missing eggs?

Easterland

Bunny is glad to be back home in Easterland. Most of the warren have been crafting delicious eggs, but some naughty rabbits have been frolicking in the chocolate river. Bunny doesn't have time to put them back to work — there's a last batch of eggs to collect before the magical adventure is over and everyone can eat chocolate happily ever after.

Can you find Bunny and the ten missing eggs?

WORKSHOP

THAT WAY

THIS WAY

FOLLOW ME

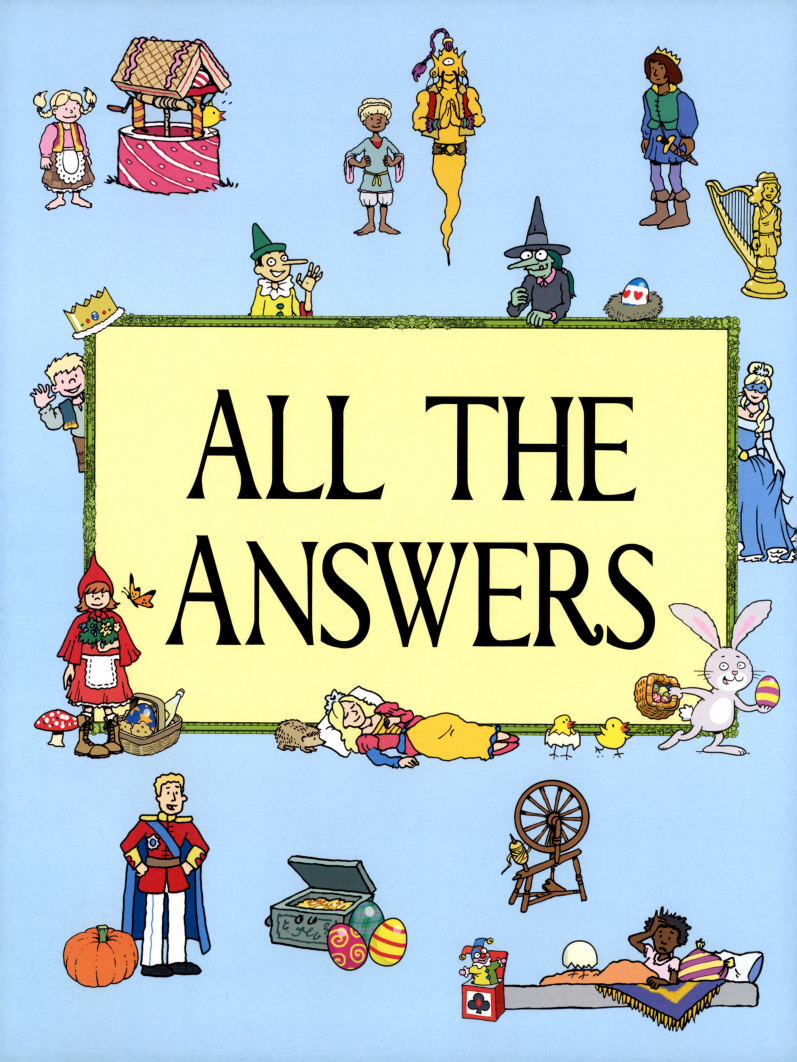

ALL THE ANSWERS

Cinderella

A clock ◯   A glass slipper ◯   Two pumpkins ◯   Two ugly sisters fighting ◯

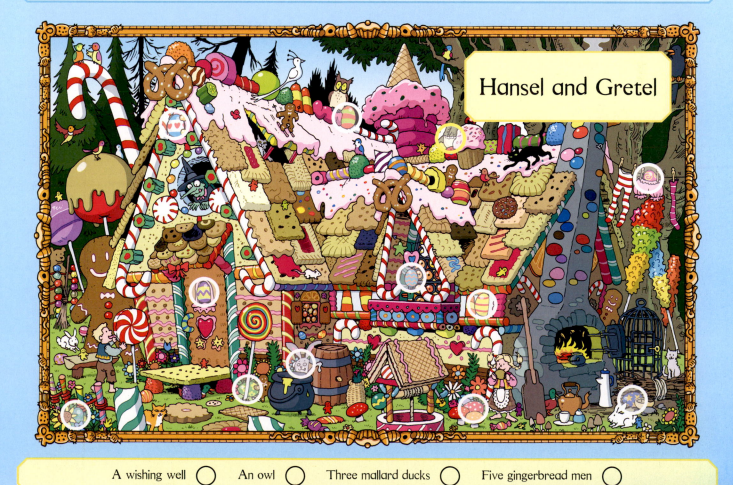

Hansel and Gretel

A wishing well ◯   An owl ◯   Three mallard ducks ◯   Five gingerbread men ◯

Snow White

A big purple pot ○   A roast chicken ○   Three squirrels ○   Seven lamps ○

The Adventures of Aladdin

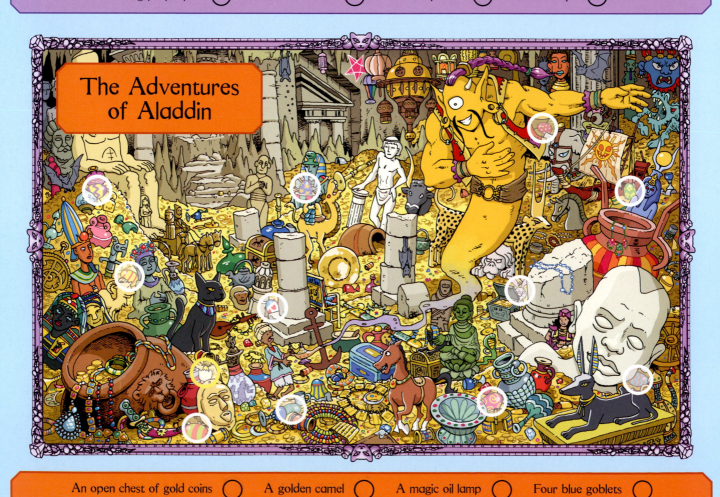

An open chest of gold coins ○   A golden camel ○   A magic oil lamp ○   Four blue goblets ○

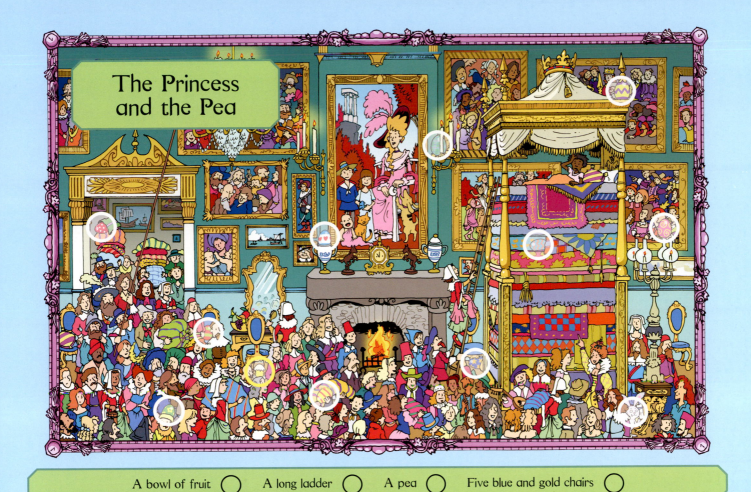

The Princess and the Pea

A bowl of fruit ◯   A long ladder ◯   A pea ◯   Five blue and gold chairs ◯

The Pied Piper of Hamelin

A basket of laundry ◯   A horse ◯   A man falling off a ladder ◯   Two wheelbarrows ◯

Sleeping Beauty

A spinning wheel ⭕   A wicked fairy ⭕   Three sleeping violinists ⭕   Five sleeping guards ⭕

Pinocchio

A cuckoo clock ⭕   A rocking horse ⭕   A wind-up ballerina ⭕   Three jars of paint ⭕

The Little Mermaid

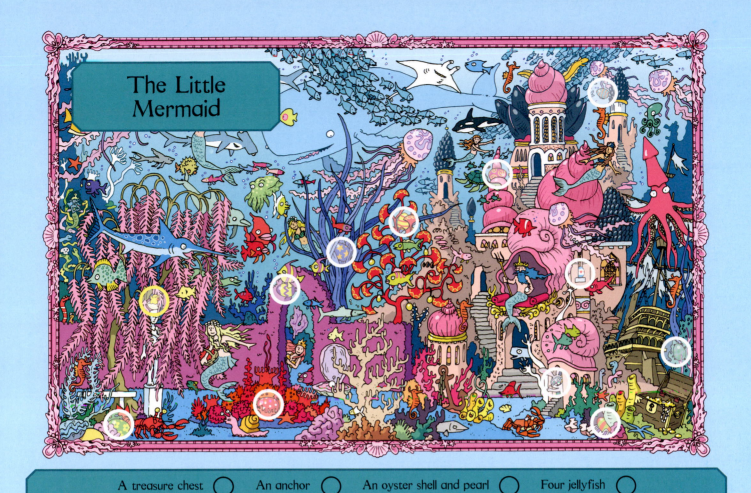

A treasure chest ◯   An anchor ◯   An oyster shell and pearl ◯   Four jellyfish ◯

The Frog Prince

A golden-boy fountain ◯   A queen ◯   Three spotty lily pads ◯   Five rose bushes ◯

Little Red Riding Hood

A bear ◯   A strawberry plant ◯   Four toadstools ◯   Seven acorns ◯

Jack and the Beanstalk

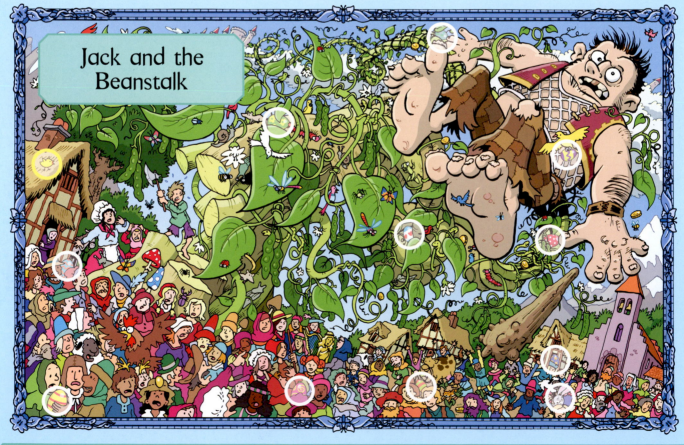

A golden harp ◯   Three ladybirds ◯   Four snakes ◯   Seven gold coins ◯

Easterland

WORKSHOP

THAT WAY

FOLLOW ME

A hedgehog ◯　A paintbrush ◯　Three lollipops ◯　Five arrow-shaped signs ◯

THE END

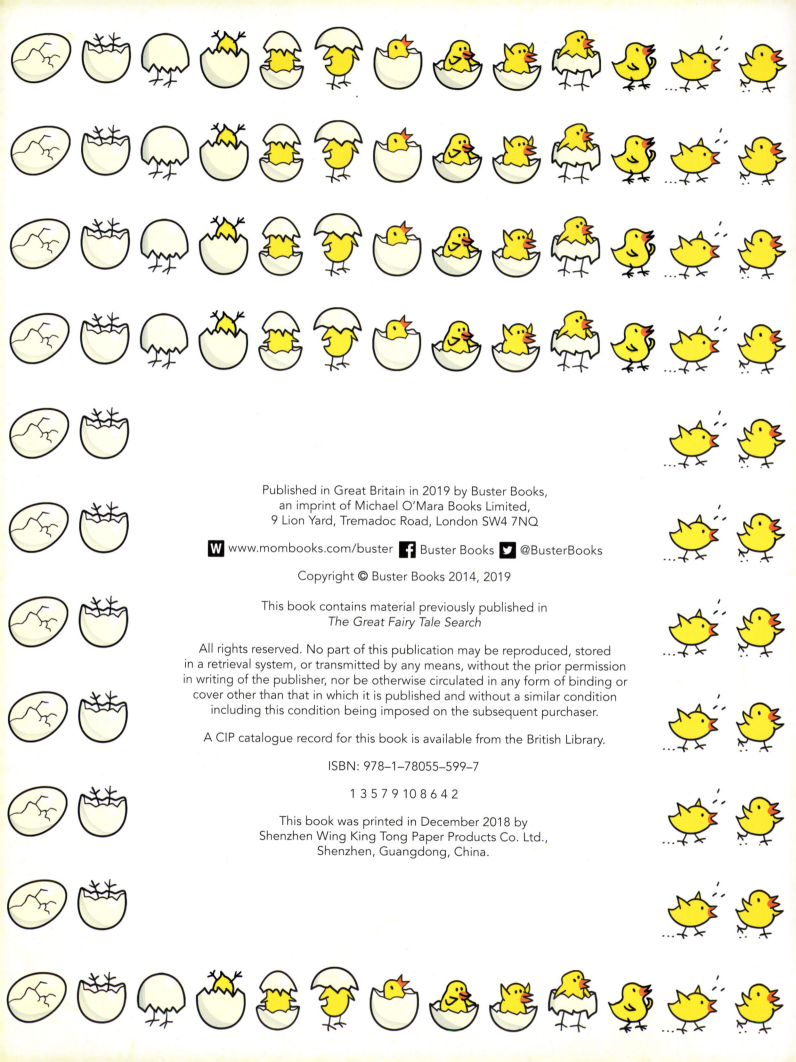

Published in Great Britain in 2019 by Buster Books,
an imprint of Michael O'Mara Books Limited,
9 Lion Yard, Tremadoc Road, London SW4 7NQ

W www.mombooks.com/buster f Buster Books 🐦 @BusterBooks

This book contains material previously published in
The Great Fairy Tale Search

A CIP catalogue record for this book is available from the British Library.

ISBN: 978–1–78055–599–7

1 3 5 7 9 10 8 6 4 2

This book was printed in December 2018 by
Shenzhen Wing King Tong Paper Products Co. Ltd.,
Shenzhen, Guangdong, China.

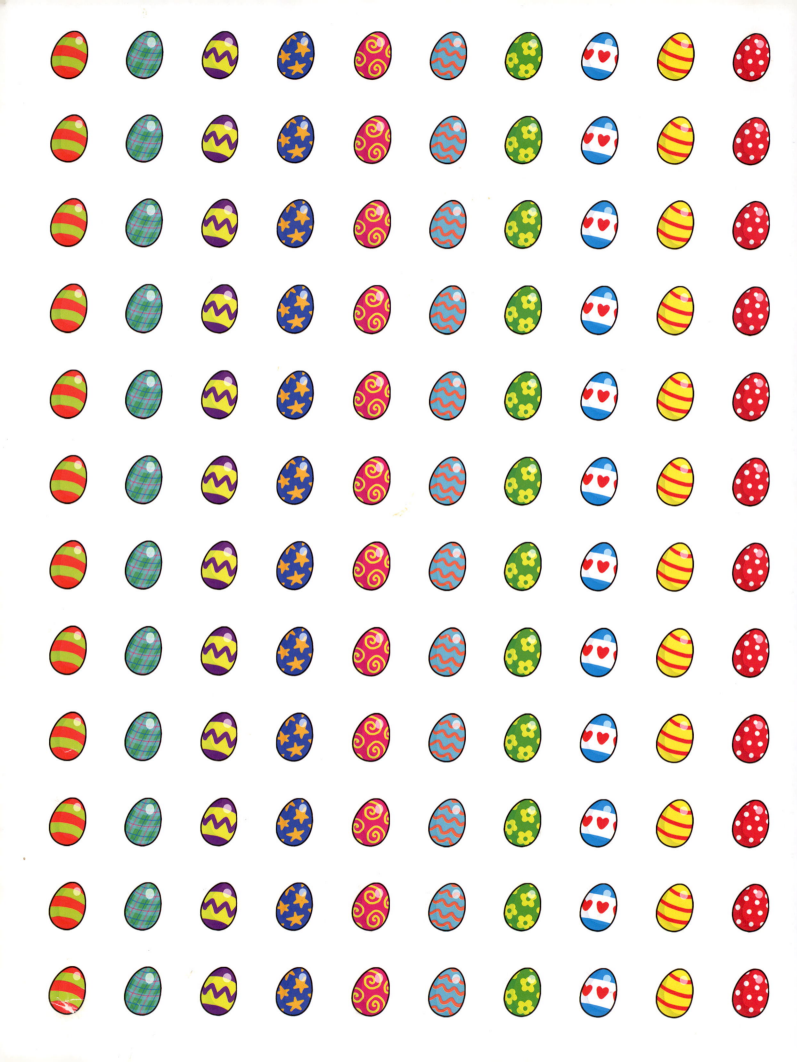

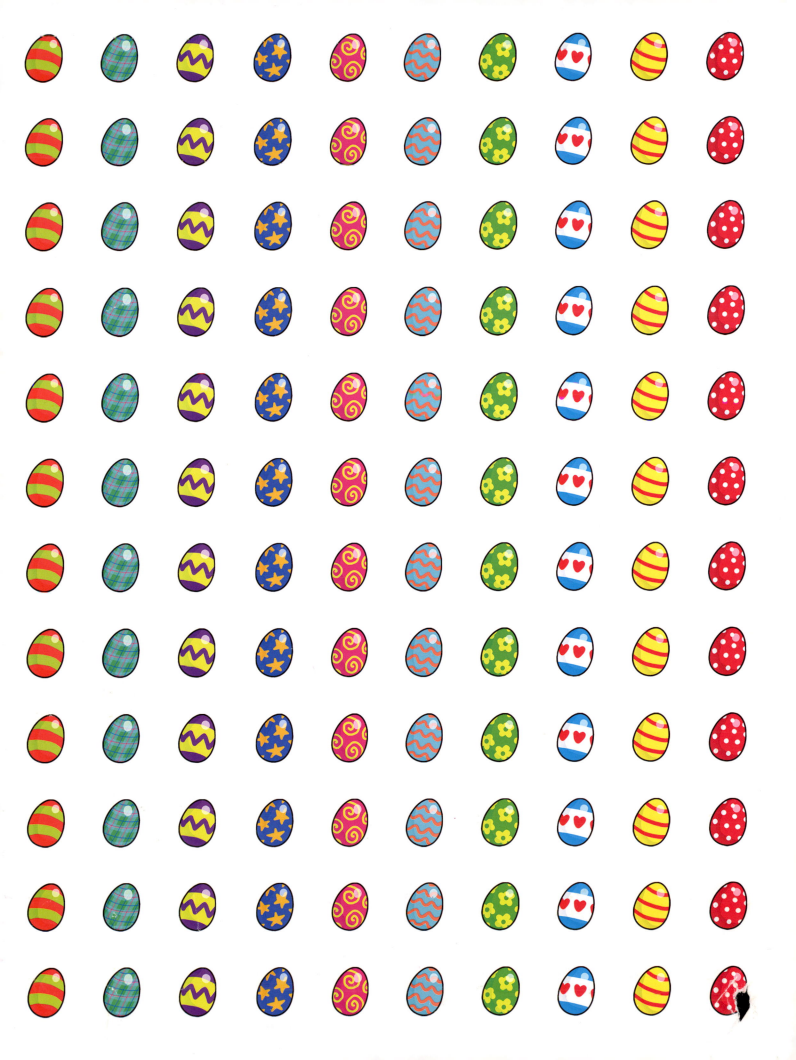